Lofty
and the Singing

Illustrations by Dynamo

EGMONT

EGMONT

We bring stories to life

First published in Great Britain 2008 by Egmont UK Limited
The Yellow Building,1 Nicholas Road, London W11 4AN

Endpapers and introductory illustrations by Craig Cameron.

HiT entertainment

ISBN 978 1 4052 4111 3

45630/4

Printed in Italy

Egmont is passionate about helping to preserve the world's remaining ancient forests.
We only use paper from legal and sustainable forest sources.

This book is made from paper certified by the Forest Stewardship Council® (FSC®),
an organisation dedicated to promoting responsible management of forest resources.
For more information on the FSC, please visit www.fsc.org. To learn more about
Egmont's sustainable paper policy, please visit www.egmont.co.uk/ethical

Farmer Pickles' pickers teach Lofty to sing. But how can Lofty be the star of the campfire sing-along if he has no time to practise?

One hot summer's day in Sunflower Valley, Bob and Farmer Pickles had a new job for the machines.

"Today, team," said Bob, "we are going to build a bunk house."

"It's a wooden house for my guests to sleep in. Here they come now!" said Farmer Pickles.

Just then, Travis arrived with three people sitting in his trailer. Lofty followed behind.

The people in the trailer were singing, and before long, Lofty joined in, too:

> "... *But the thing that I love pickin'*
> *I could pick a ton or two,*
> *Is a great big field of sunflowers*
> *Every picker knows it's true!*"

The machines looked at Lofty, amazed.

"Wow," said Roley, "we've never heard you sing before, Lofty. You're great!"

"Meet Mickey, Vicky and Ricky!" said Lofty, rolling up beside the trailer. "They're the pickers helping with the sunflower harvest. And they're great singers, too!"

The pickers began to sing again.

Lofty smiled. "They've been teaching me songs all morning!" he said.

"Well, you can teach us a song or two while we work," laughed Bob.

The machines sorted the logs for the bunk house, while the pickers prepared to set off to the fields.

"... *Lift the logs and lay them down. All day long!*" sang Lofty.

"You're doing a grand job, Lofty," said Vicky. "Will you be the star of our sing-along around the campfire tonight?"

Lofty was surprised. "Me, the star?" he said. "Oh, er, thanks very much ..."

Suddenly, Lofty didn't feel like singing any more. Dizzy saw that he looked sad.

"Cheer up, Lofty," said Dizzy. "You're going to be the star!"

"I do like singing, but not on my own. What if I'm no good?" Lofty worried.

Dizzy smiled, kindly. "You just need to practise. Ha-ha-ha, I'll help!" She twirled around on the spot. "Let's go and find somewhere quiet."

Dizzy sped off, but before Lofty could follow, Bob and Wendy called him over.

"Come on, Lofty," said Bob. "Time to get the walls of this bunk house up!"

"We can't do it without you," said Wendy.

Lofty rolled sadly towards the pile of logs. He couldn't practise his singing now. Poor Lofty felt very worried indeed.

Just then, Lofty's talkie-talkie crackled. It was Dizzy. "I'm at Mr Beasley's yurt!" she said. "It's nice and quiet, come quickly!"

So Lofty put down his logs and raced off before anybody noticed.

"I wish I were the star!" said Dizzy, when Lofty arrived. "OK, let's get singing …"

But before Lofty had sung a note, his talkie-talkie crackled again. It was Bob calling him back to the bunk house.

So Lofty trundled back to see Bob. "I'll never be the star if I don't practise," he worried.

"There you are, Lofty!" said Bob. "We can't build this roof without your help."

Lofty lifted the wood for Wendy, while Bob hammered on the roof.

"We'll soon have this job finished," smiled Bob. "Then it'll be sing-along time around the campfire!"

Dizzy called Lofty on his talkie-talkie. She'd found another quiet place.

Lofty crept away again to meet Dizzy, who was hiding by some tall sunflowers. "No one will disturb us here!" she said.

But, just then, the pickers appeared through the sunflowers. "Looking forward to tonight, Lofty?" smiled Mickey.

Before Lofty could answer, Wendy was calling him back to the bunk house.

"We'll never get the job done if you keep disappearing!" laughed Wendy, when Lofty arrived back at the bunk house.

"We wouldn't want to miss the sing-along," added Scoop. "You're the star, after all!"

Lofty said nothing. Bob, Wendy and the machines worked quickly to fit the bunks into place. Soon, the work was done.

"We did it!" cheered Bob. "Now for some singing fun."

As the sun set, everyone gathered around the finished bunk house. Lofty looked very worried.

"Hi, Lofty!" said Mickey. "Are you excited?"

"Not really," cried Lofty. "I'm scared. I don't want to be the star and sing on my own."

Mickey smiled. "Oh, Lofty," he said, "you don't have to sing on your own!"

Lofty was puzzled. "I don't?" he said.

"We sing songs about who we meet," said Ricky. "Tonight's song is all about you."

Lofty had been worrying for nothing all day! Now he was excited about the song.

The pickers started to sing:
"*We all said to Bob, pick Lofty for the job!*"

"Next time you're worried about something, Lofty, talk to us," said Bob.

"I will," Lofty laughed. "I'm Lofty the star!"

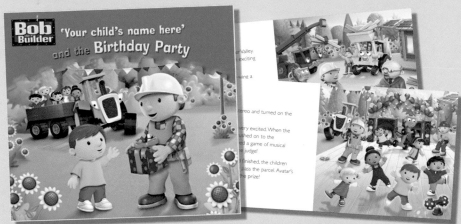